The Darkest Hours II

Howling Violins

Cameron Rue

Chapter 1

There Jeff was, sitting in the car peering behind

him, through the rearview mirror waiting for the

apartments building's front door to open.

He has been there for three hours now. The urge

to just shatter the front glass door and rush into make his

move was intensifying.

"This waiting shit sucks balls," he muttered to

himself and grabbed him a cigarette from the pack in his

pocket. Just as he was getting ready to spark up, the door opened.

Jeff speedily stepped out of the vehicle revealing his two hundred and seventy-two-pound muscular body. Slowly he approached the person that just exited the building and shouted, "Hey you!"

The person promptly noticed Jeff's size and muttered, "Fuck," and took off running.

Jeff stopped walking. He glanced around for a rock.

Once he founded it he hurled it at the runner, knocking the man unconscious. He wasted no time in throwing the one hundred and forty-six-pound man over his right shoulder and placing him in the trunk of the car. He

drove to a secluded area and opened the trunk. He sat on

the back bumper and smoked himself a few cigarettes

until the man awakened.

"Good evening," Jeff welcomed.

The scared, man attempted to flee and Jeff grabbed

him by the neck with one hand and pulled him out while

saying, "That didn't work last time what makes you think

is going to now?"

The man couldn't reply, so Jeff loosen his grip a bit. He felt the man swallow and then tightened his grip again while asking, "When are you going to have Johnny's money?"

He waited till the man's face turned purple and then he loosened his grip again this time allowing the man to reply, "I swear I will have it tomorrow."

Jeff scowled and was getting to squeeze the life out of the man. However, Jeff's phone began to sing 'Hit me baby one more time,' by Britney Spears.

It was his daughter Chloe and for her to be calling, it has got to be important. He dropped the man back in the trunk and slammed it shut. He answered and immediately she demanded to be picked up from school.

"Why pumpkin? Did you miss your bus again?" He asked in his sweetest voice.

"No dad," she snapped, "I had detention!"

"For what?" He scowled.

"I punched this bitch on the nose!" She replied.

"Be there in ten minutes," he confirmed, "and on the way home we are going to have a long talk."

Chapter 2

Jeff opened the trunk and gave the man twenty-four hours. He then punched him on the side of the face, knocking out three teeth and placing him back unconscious. He awakened on the park bench across his apartment building.

Jeff was on his way to pick up Chloe, when his boss Johnny called.

"So, did you get the money from Victor?" He exclaimed.

"I gave him twenty-four hours," Jeff replied while putting the phone on speaker so he can focus on the road.

"What!" Johnny screamed.

Jeff didn't say a word. He heard Johnny grunt and there was what seemed like a long pause.

Jeff broke the silence, "I got to pick up my daughter."

Johnny cleared his throat and then ordered, "On your way there swing by Viola Howls. Old bag late on her rent."

"Yes Boss," Jeff replied and they both hung up.

Jeff turned on the radio and enjoyed the smooth sound of jazz. He was so into it he drove by Viola Howls, saw the eighty-two-year-old sitting on her rocking chair on the front porch. He quickly slammed his foot on the brakes, placed the gear onto reverse and pulled up in front the house. He stepped out of the car and then noticed she was gone.

"It isn't no way in hell she moved that fast," he said to himself.

He walked onto the porch and then heard the crackling of the crow sitting on the bare crippling tree to his right. He was getting to knock on the door when suddenly Chloe called again.

"Shit!" He expressed.

He had forgotten all about her.

Viola Howls would have to wait for now.

Chapter 3

"I'm two minutes away," Jeff answered. "I'm have been out here for almost an hour," Chloe snapped.

"Well maybe next time you'll think twice about putting your hands on somebody else," he argued and hung up just as he was pulling up in front of the school.

There she was sitting on the steps looking as gloom as ever. She stood up and walked towards the car. As she sat on the front passenger seat she rolled her eyes while placing her bookbag over her lap.

He accelerated while she closed the door and stared out of the side window. He was going to say something but then his phone went off.

"Hello," he answered.

"Did you get my rent from Viola Howls?" Johnny asked.

"Yeah, I'm swinging by there now," he lied and quickly made a U-turn.

"Make it happen," Johnny ordered and hung up.

Within a few minutes Jeff was parked, back at Viola's house. He exited the vehicle and immediately Chloe let out a loud groan and then uttered, "I want to go home."

Jeff heard her and whispered, "Too bad."

He stepped onto the porch and was getting ready to knock when suddenly a raspy high pitch voice asked, "How may I help you? Young man?"

He looked to where it had come from and saw Viola standing with her cane to his right below the crippling tree.

"Where is Johnny's rent?" Jeff exclaimed.

She gradually started walking towards him while glancing down. When she became exhausted, she stopped and raised her head up to get a better look at him while replying, "He will get it when I have it."

"You are not fooling me grandma. I know about your inheritance," Jeff informed.

Viola curled her bottom peeling lip downward to the left while scowling, "So that gives you guys the right to raise my rent?"

Jeff approached her and stood right in front of her.

He looked down at her and stated, "I'm giving you one hour to have all the money plus an extra four grands."

"And if I refuse!" She challenged with her eyes wide opened.

"Oh, you going to find out." He threatened and left

it at that.

He jumped back into his car and made a K-turn

while the whole time Viola just watched with a frown on

her face. Chloe made eye contact and felt a cold shiver

run down her spine. "Something isn't right," she

whispered.

Chapter 4

Jeff dropped Chloe at the house and proceeded to

head back to Viola's.

Chloe watched as his car disappeared into the

horizon, having a feeling she was never going to see him

again.

Jeff was twenty feet away from Viola's when all

the sudden he heard an explosion. His steering wheel

trembled and the front left side of the car began to make

loud thud noises.

He pulled over to examine what just occurred. He figured he had flat so he grabbed the spare, jack and tire-iron.

He made sure that the car was in "park" and the emergency brake was set. He then loosened the flat-tire with the tire-iron.

He then moved the jack underneath the car, raised the vehicle until the flat tire was completely off the ground. Once this was done, he finished removing the

loose lugs.

He then saw what had caused it. At first, he didn't

know what to make of it. Then after closer inspection he

realized it was a bird's beak with no body. Little did he

know that the crows' infested with fleas' carcass was

resting behind the right back tire trembling like it was

being electrocuted.

"How can a bird beak do this?" He asked himself,

being too vein to comprehend dark forces at hand.

He neverminded it for now and position the spare tire over the wheel studs, screwed back in the lugs and then carefully lowered the jack.

He removed it and tightened each lug.

Just as he was done he felt a cold light breeze. It caused a cold shiver to run down his spine.

He put the bad feeling aside and carried the tools including flat tire and placed them into the trunk.

He went back inside his car, released the brakes

and placed the gear on drive when out of nowhere

Johnny hit his phone.

"I'm at Viola's" Jeff lied.

"Forget that for now. I got more pressing matters,"

Johnny informed sounding extremely concerned.

Jeff rolled his eyes, thinking, "Here we go again."

And Johnny continued, "Go see Chico and his

gang they just called and threatened me."

He cleared his throat and Jeff could hear him sparking up a cigar.

"Go break their skulls!" Johnny finished saying while exhaling a thick cloud of smoke.

"I'm on it boss." Jeff obeyed.

Viola Howls watched him from her upstairs bedroom window, drive by her house and make a right on the next block.

She looked at her wrist watch and smiled, then said

while giggling in a low tone of voice, "The curse has

begun?"

Chapter 5

Jeff made another right on the following block. Five lights down the road and the gang came into view.

Hanging in front of the chop-chop garage as usual. They noticed his car approaching and ran inside the garage.

"Run little bitches," Jeff shouted and pulled up right in front.

Immediately ten gang members stampeded out of the garage, some carrying wooden bats and other crowbars. Without giving him a chance to get out, they jumped on top of his car and started wailing on it like wild baboons.

Their terror effort worked.

"Fuck!" Jeff screamed and slammed the gas pedal to the floor.

All but Chico jumped off or fell off the car.

Chico, remained on the top hood attempting to put the crowbar through.

So, Jeff did the expected. He slammed on the brakes attempting to throw Chico onto the black top.

However, Chico had already placed the tool

halfway through and he used it as support to remain, but

it caused his shoulders to dislocate.

He had no choice but to let go and hit the black

top left side first forcing the shoulder back in, then

rolling in mid-air landing on his right side doing the

same.

When Jeff noticed Chico was standing up without

what appeared to be a scratch. The enforcer quickly

placed the car on reverse. He stepped on the gas pedal

and then he heard his worse fears clearly coming out of

Chico mouth, "I know where you live with that sweet ass

daughter of yours, Chloe."

Chapter 6

After hearing what Chico had just blurted, Jeff wasted no time in braking. Something had taken over him. He stormed out of the car ignoring all warnings signs *that his path had been* cursed and headed for Chico.

Chico decided to meet him halfway, creating a diversion so Jeff wouldn't realize that the gang was going to ambush him from behind.

Before he could even crack Chico skull with his

huge fist, he felt an intense pain on the back of his head.

He turned around and saw that a gang member was

tightly holding onto a broken wooden bat.

He grabbed it off him and shoved its splintered

edges into his abdomen.

Chico took advantage of the situation by

penetrating the crowbar into Jeff's upper back.

Jeff growled while turning around and colliding

his fist with Chico's right side of the face. The impact

dislocated Chico's jaw causing his chin to move three inches to the left.

When Chico collapsed onto the ground the rest of the gang quickly retreated.

Jeff pulled the crowbar out of his back and threw on top of Chico who was now unconscious. Now he heard the sirens approaching fast. So, he took his wounded ass back into his damaged car. However, he wasn't sure if he should have gone to the hospital. He was so spaced out he couldn't drive. So, he pulled over and glanced to his left and saw Viola revealing a devilish grin right in front of her house.

"How the fuck did I get here?" He uttered.

Chapter 7

"Has an hour come to past?" Viola happily shouted.

Jeff wasn't in a mood for this shit. He stepped out of the car while snarling, "You want some of me? Old bag!"

She grew an even bigger grin as she replied, "From the looks of it, someone ripped you apart from what I can see, so what is there left for me?"

Jeff made his hands into fists while growling,

"Enough!"

Without a second to waste, he charged, crossing

the street gunning right for her.

Suddenly everything seemed to move in slow

motion.

He could hear his cellphone, which was still in the

car ringing the 'Britney Spears' song, 'Baby Hit Me One

More Time.'

It was Chloe sitting at home looking through the

window at the sky. Watching the dark clouds come in.

She had a bad feeling.

So, she kept ringing his phone. However, even

though he could hear it loud and clear he had other things

in his mind.

He was so focused on Viola that he didn't see the

van coming until it was too late. On impact, he flew on

top of the front hood. Still going upward shattering the

windshield before rolling to the very top hood and falling

off its side.

He hit the black top face first and used the last of his strength to turn his head just in time to witness Chico's gang exiting the van carrying metal bats.

"For Chico," they shouted waving their weapons in the air.

Jeff knew this was the end. He tried lifting himself up for one last brawl, but he didn't have the energy.

He closed his eyes whispering, "Chloe."

Chapter 8

As the dark clouds now hovered over Chloe's

house, they released golf ball size hail. She immediately

jumped away from the window, tripped and banged her

head against the coffee table.

She saw darkness for a few seconds as she stood

on her knees.

Now she felt it!

Her daddy was gone!

She opened her eyes and mouth wide opened. Tears smeared her dark blue eyeliner down her face and she followed it with her nails, penetrating the skin while all the lights in the house flickered off.

This intensified her fear and she attempted to run out of the room, but hit the wall head first.

She felt something then attempting to take over her mind.

"Daddy please no!" She cried and stood up.

She placed her palms against the wall and used them as a guide to head up stairs.

Once she reached the top, the light in front of her came on while the rest of the house remained in darkness.

As she walked by it she heard a raspy high pitch voice say, "Remember!"

Now the light went out and the one further ahead of her flickered on.

"Remember," the voice continued.

"Daddy no!" She cried and proceeded ahead while the light behind her went out and the one around the corner in the bathroom came on.

She went in there as the voice continued to haunt her.

Finally, she fought back by shouting" Nothing happened!"

"Then be it," the voice growled and the light shut off leaving her in darkness again.

She felt a gentle breeze sweep over her feet and she burst into more cries.

"What is it going to be?" The voice softly asked.

Chloe then sobbed, "He did it."

The light came back on.

She held onto the sink and looked at the mirror.

Suddenly she felt ashamed and confused.

She now had two memories of her past. The one

she lived and what the darkness wanted her to believe.

She walked towards the shower and turned it on.

In her warped mind, she had just passed out again from

eating the drugged dinner her father just served her.

She was now old enough to know what he had

being doing. The touching, with him softly saying, "I

love you," then penetrating her, thrusting, releasing all

his stress inside her.

She immediately entered the ice-cold shower. She scrubbed her whole body with her nails until she bled.

She felt the warmness of her blood as it gradually dribbled down her body. Her stomach then began to be tightened. She gasped as it condensed inward.

The pain moved downward.

All the sudden it eased away as the spiders finally burst out of her vagina and went down the drain.

She turned the water off and the spiders that survived the downward spiral now crawled up to her feet.

She felt them coming up her legs and looked down. She exploded into high pitch screams while waving them off.

She slipped and hit her head against the edge of the tub.

Chapter 9

Chloe awakened on the living room couch. She released a sigh of relief, understanding it was all one big nightmare.

She glanced out of the window, the stormed had come to past, but what about her father.

She grabbed her phone and dialed.

"Hello!" He answered, sounding like he had just awakened.

She was so happy to hear his voice.

"When are you coming home?"

He paused for a minute.

He was confused.

He didn't know where he was.

So, he sat up and that's when he saw her.

"Let me call you right back," he calmly said and hung up to focus on the matter at hand.

He tried standing up and Viola in a sweet raspy voice said, "Now be careful you took a good beaten. I did the best I can."

Without listening to another word, he stood up. That's when he felt that something wasn't right. He wasn't the same. He rushed to the nearest mirror while grunting, "Where am I?"

He glanced at her who just pointed straight ahead at the front door. He ran for it and once he was outside, he saw that he had been inside her house the whole time.

He rushed across the street to his damaged car. He

examined his face and all that he was able too, through

the door side mirror. Everything seemed to be okay, but

he felt different.

He didn't have a scratch on him.

"What did she do to me?"

His phone rang again, he had forgotten he had it in

his hand the entire time.

"Hey boss," he answered.

"Good job! "Johnny happily shouted and continued, "Don't know how you fucking did it man! You must have scared them good! Chico lieutenant came by they gave me every penny they owed plus an extra four grands for my troubles."

Jeff couldn't believe what he was hearing something wasn't right, but he let him talk.

"They left you a gift in a sealed box too. I have it on top of my desk so if you swing by don't forget to grab it. I'm going out to the club to party. Is been one hell of a day."

Jeff silently agreed.

Johnny hung up and Jeff just stood there baffled as ever. He glanced behind him at Violas house. There she stood on her front porch leaning her small scrawny body against her wooden cane with a devilish grin on her face.

"What the fuck you do to me!" He growled.

"Now why be so ungrateful after I just saved your life from that gang?" She happily informed, "Now is not my fault that all the dirty deeds you had done took you into hell. I tried my best but a claimed soul can't run free forever."

"What the fuck are you talking about!" He screamed.

Suddenly her eyes became pitch black and her mouth dropped open as a swarm of flies exited and then she growled, "He is coming for you!"

The swarm of flies gathered in front of him to form a human figure.

He took a swing at its head smashing the flies and revealing an open cavity. This startled the creature giving Jeff the opportunity to strike again. This time putting his whole hand through its torso.

The creature exploded into ashes, covering Jeff

and half of his car.

When all the grey smoke cleared he focused back

on Viola, however she was gone!

"You are not getting away that easy," he blurted and ran

across the street and onto her porch.

He banged on her door while screaming, "Open the fuck

up!"

It seemed to fall onto deaf ears. So, he was getting

ready to kick down the door when suddenly it lightly

came open.

He pushed it open all the way and charged in.

He stopped in the middle of what now was an

empty room, when just moments ago had furniture.

"Not what you expect," he heard her say.

He looked around for her, "Where the fuck is you?"

He searched every room upstairs and down. All

were empty of her and furniture. He walked out of the

house and his phone rang. It was Chloe and he sent her to voicemail.

Meanwhile Chloe stepped onto her house front porch, "Where are you?"

That awful feeling haunted her again. Something wasn't right. She was getting ready to head back inside and that's when she heard the crackling of the crow up on the telephone pole. She made eye contact. She recognized those eyes.

"That old lady," she whispered.

Jeff was getting ready to head back inside when abruptly the door slammed shut. He turned the knob but it wouldn't budge.

So, he prepared to kick the door down and his phone rang again. He knew by the ring tone that it was Chloe.

"What!" He snarled then heard her cry, "Daddy please come home I'm scared!"

He paused for a moment, eyes becoming watery, couldn't stand still, hearing her beg. He had enough, he came back to his senses and stated, "I'm on my way!"

Chapter 10

In seven minutes, he was parked in the garage of

his house.

Chloe heard the car door shut and rushed out to

greet him in a hug.

He happily welcomed it and then froze when he

heard her say, "I thought I would never see you again!"

How did she know? Unless!

He brushed her aside and rushed inside the house while she stood there crying, "Daddy!"

He looked in every room, closet and corner. He ended up back at the front door as Chloe was just coming back in.

"Where is she?" He growled.

Chloe slowly turned around and pointed at the crow who was just quietly standing on the pole.

It noticed him and flew away.

He had enough of this shit. He was getting ready to

go back to Violas house, but Chloe grabbed

him by the hand and begged, "Daddy please no!"

He looked at her soaked with tears face as she

continued, "Let it go!"

Maybe he should listen, but he couldn't let go of

the feeling that something wasn't right with him.

Either way he took her advice.

He closed the door and went into the kitchen. He opened the top cabinet above the sink and grabbed the unopened bottle of 'Jack Daniels.'

He hadn't touch a drink since his wife Teressa had moved onto a better place.

Two hours later after consuming half of the bottle, he decided to take a shower. He had the water on full blown hot and for some odd reason it still felt cold to him.

Realization that he can't no longer feel,

What's wrong?

Can this be for real?

Desire for all of it to be done!

Is this the ultimate price he has to pay?

He shall see, tomorrow is another day.

Chapter 11

Jeff awakened on his bed and placed his bare feet on the floor. That's when he noticed his skin complexion had changed.

He thought no more of it. For today was a new day. Waking up optimistic always had helped him in the past.

He had already decided he was going to forget about Viola and the stupid curse!

He walked into the bathroom and took a leak.

Afterwards he approached the sink and washed his face.

Once he was done he glanced himself in the mirror and was horrified at the color of his skin.

He couldn't believe it, so he washed his face again and glanced back at the mirror.

It was for sure now. His body was swelling and was the color grey. His was dead.

Maybe is just a dream,

Witnessing his own very decay,

Bursting into a deep tone scream.

How can he face his daughter looking this way!

Already a fucked up day!

He stormed out of the bathroom and back into his

room. He tripped over a shoe and hit the corner of the

lamp desk mouth first.

He didn't feel anything, but did witnessed all his

top and bottom teeth scattering on the floor.

He brought himself back to his feet and then went to retreat every single tooth. Once he had them all he went back into the bathroom.

He attempted to place them back into the gums, but ran into a problem. It wasn't possible, but he had to figure out something.

He couldn't let Chloe see him this way. She was afraid enough of Viola. Now him? No way in hell. He had to do something, but what? How can he put his teeth back in?

Suddenly, he heard her shout from downstairs, "Daddy is that you?"

He quickly slammed shut the door and replied, "Yes, honey!"

He heard footsteps approaching and then she asked from right outside the door, "What's that smell?"

"Shit," he murmured.

She sighed and then exclaimed, "Did something die up here?"

"Just using the bathroom baby," he shouted while going into the bottom cabinet and grabbing the air freshener. He sprayed as she was saying, "Well, I got to go."

Shit! Was she just going to stand there and wait? "Well, go downstairs, start that coffee. I be out in a jiffy!" He hollered.

He crept by the door and listened for her to leave. Once he was sure she was gone, he stormed out and locked himself in the bedroom. Should he remain there until he, decompose completely? What the fuck should he do?

He sat on the edge of his bed and thought about it. He then heard her come back upstairs.

"Damn, dad it stinks up here!" She stated.

He stared at the bedroom door.

He had the feeling she was just going to walk in and just out of nowhere his phone rang.

It was his boss Johnny. He didn't want to answer it, but as an impulse he did and Johnny didn't even let him get a word out before ordering, "On your way up here get my money from Victor and swing by Viola's."

Shit! Jeff had forgotten, he had given Victor twenty four hours. His time was up….

However, he was getting ready to tell Johnny he quit, but before he could the phone cut off.

Two seconds later…..

"Dad," said Chloe, from near the bedroom door. Jeff quickly hid underneath the bed covers and replied, "Yes, honey!"

He waited for her to open the door, but instead she just said, "I'm on my way to school. I have to stay late for detention again, can you pick me up?"

Now he knew damn well he wasn't going to be able, but he lied, "Yeah!"

"Okay I love you," she said and without waiting for a respond was out of the house.

As she walked down the street to the corner, she failed to notice, the 2016, white Mercedes Benz with tinted window sedan, parked in front of the house.

However, the driver noticed her. He leaned back in the seat, just in case she turned around.

He watched as she stood on the corner and waited for the bus. He felt a little more comfortable now that he was sure he wasn't spotted. So, he took a quick glance the front door of the house. He needed to get in there, but breaking into someone's domain wasn't his thing.

Especially a cursed someone…..

Nevertheless, he might have no other option. He

waited until the bus pulled up in front of Chloe and then

prepared to exit the vehicle, when suddenly his phone

rang.

"Yes," he answered in a firm tone of voice.

"Forget him," a female voice softly said from the
other line, "Focus on her."

"Understood, ma'am," he replied and started the
engine.

Chapter 12

Once Jeff was sure Chloe was on her way to

school, he jumped out of the bed and rushed back inside

the bathroom. He couldn't help but to look at his

decaying face in the mirror.

What was he going to do? How could he explain

this? There was no other choice. He had to confront

Viola and have her remove this curse.

He wasted no time in completely dressing with

long sleeves and pants. His face however, would have to

remain exposed for now. But he did put on a cap and thick sunglasses. Within just a few minutes he was driving down the street to confront the old hag.

Who said she was going to be home? Last time she pulled a disappearing act. Still, he had to try. He basically had no other choice.

Just as he was pulling up, he spotted her, standing, curled forward, leaning against her cane, below the crippling tree.

She saw him and didn't seem to care, waived at him, like nothing had happened the day before. Maybe it was a new day after all.

He parked the car and cautiously exited, not wanting to spook her off. He gently closed the door and she softly asked, "Different attitude today, young man?"

Damn, he wanted to knock her, the fuck out, so bad... But he had to keep his cool. She was the only one that could take away his curse.

He gradually approached her and in her sweetest voice she made aware, "You don't have to be afraid of me. There is nothing I can do to you, that hasn't been done already."

Damn, she had mouth on her... Bitch still instigating him...

Stay cool, stay cool….

"What do I have to do, for you to remove this curse?" He just blankly said it.

Silence conquered the air as she stared at him, with a big devilish grin for a good ten seconds which seemed to be a life time, when all the sudden she asked, "How is that boss of yours, Johnny?"

"What!" Jeff scowled, "You want me to take care of him?"

He would do anything to rid of this curse.

He waited for what seemed to take another life time until she responded in a high pitch giggly voice, "Let me think about it!"

"Think about it!" Jeff growled, "What the fuck is there to think about?"

"Apparently, you have never been curse before," she happily stated.

His eyes opened wide as he shouted, "What type of fucking question is that?" Then he mocked, "Apparently you haven't been curse before!"

He noticed by the look on her face, she was getting

some type of high of shit. So, he lowered his tone and

calmly stated, "No! I have never been cursed before and

to say kindly never met anyone that has either."

She let him have a gentle smile and then said,

"Come back tomorrow."

Jeff made his hands into fists.

"I don't fucking have till tomorrow bitch! Can't

you see I'm fucking decomposing?" He growled.

She stood straight up and appeared to grow taller.

She then gave him the gesture as though she was playing

a violin and then BAM! She exploded into a swarm of

crows......

Chapter 13

The white Mercedes Benz, parked in front of

Chloe's school, just as she was exiting the bus.

The driver rested back on the seat, once again

concealing himself. He was trying his hardest not to

make eye contact with her. All he had to do was observed

and report, which was pretty, easy. He was better off

doing this, then putting the curse father out of his misery.

Killing wasn't really his thing. That belonged more

to his boss, if needed. However, things been apocalyptic

for some odd reason, so he had to pick up some of the

slack. He was just praying that little ole' Chloe wasn't

cursed, for if so, it would be much harder killing a child

and he sure as hell wasn't up for it. Only way that could

change, was if he, found the spell-caster first. Only time

would tell…

He waited there all the way until school let out and

an extra hour, watching her sit there on the curve, waiting

just like him, but for what though?

She kept calling somebody. Who though?

He called his boss.

"Yes, Ivan," Sophia answered.

"Can you get technical support to wire Subject

67's cellular phone?" Ivan requested.

"Okay. Give me five minutes," she replied and

hung up.

He placed his phone on the dash-board and put it

on speaker phone. Then went back to watch Chloe, or as

she was labeled, *Subject 67*.

Before he knew, he heard rabbling through his

phone, then static, then a voice, "Daddy but you said you

was going to be here."

"Honey, I know, but something really important has come up," Jeff replied, "Call the UBER, I will pay for it."

Did Ivan hear that correctly, a cab? This was his time to make the move......

Chapter 14

Just as Chloe hung up, with Jeff, Johnny called him. He sounded enraged, screaming at him, regarding the uncollected debt from Victor.

Jeff had bigger shit to deal with and for all he knew he might have to kill Johnny tomorrow, in order for Viola to remove the curse.

Johnny continued ranting, throwing all types of stuff in his office. Finally, grabbed the package meant for Jeff. Without a second thought he threw it across the office.

The box crushed on impact and one of its corners busted open. A thick dark red liquid poured out of there. "What the fuck," Johnny express as it drew his interest.

He placed the phone on top of the desk and then grabbed the box. Through its opening he could see what appeared be a human eye starring back at him.

He quickly dropped the box and it now fully opened revealing Victor's head.

"Sick mother fucker!" He screamed.

He grabbed the phone and began swearing at Jeff, whom of course had no idea of what Johnny was talking about.

Jeff hung up on him. Once Johnny took notice he

called again and Jeff just sent him straight to voicemail.

Johnny called again! Same thing voicemail!

"Bastard!" He growled and threw the phone

against the wall.

When he realized what he had just done, he

grabbed his car keys stormed out of the building.

"You want to ignore me mother fucker?" He said

out loud to himself and kept on going. "Got people

sending you heads of my clients that haven't paid me yet.

I'm fucking losing money! So now you going to pay!"

He entered his car, placed the key in the ignition

and started it up.

Before peeling out, he checked the glove

compartment to make sure the Glock was still in there.

"You going to pay me bastard," he said as sped to Jeff's

house.

Meanwhile Ivan took his phone off speaker and pretended to be the UBER cab.

He picked up Chloe and as she sat in the back seat he focused on the road as well as her energy. He could feel the curse, but it wasn't as strong as his boss Sophia had expected. So, he now knew Chloe wasn't the spell caster, but also not its intended victim.

He felt relieved now, that he didn't have to kill her, but felt sympathetic that she would have to live out the rest of her life wondering what had happened to her

father. He suddenly slammed his foot on the brakes as

Johnny cut him off, speeding towards Jeff's house.

Ivan turned to face Chloe, "Are you okay?"

"That's my dad's boss!" She cried.

Then that feeling came over her again. Something

bad was going to happen.

"I got to home!" She shrieked.

Ivan felt it too and without hesitation he slammed

his foot on the gas pedal. Before he knew it, he was

braking again this time right behind Johnny's car that was

parked in the middle of the road in front of Viola's house.

Chapter 15

Ivan watched as Johnny exited the car holding onto

the Glock.

"Where the fuck is my money!" He shouted at

Viola who was standing, leaning her body against the

cane below the crippling tree to the right of her house.

"I have been expecting you," she happily replied.

"Go please!" Chloe begged Ivan, but he couldn't, there was no way around.

"You got my money?" Johnny scowled.

Viola stood straight with her hands off the cane and pretended to play a violin for six seconds and then growled in a demonic tone, "Hear them howl!"

Her mouth dropped open, until her chin touched the ground.

Her tongue rolled out of her mouth like a carpet. Then her esophagus expanded as she vomited one huge wolf.

It charged at Johnny who fired three consecutive rounds as another crawled out of her mouth.

Ivan quickly placed the gear on reverse and slammed his foot on the gas pedal. As the first wolf went down, Johnny shot the other while retreating towards his car.

However, a third and fourth wolf came out of her mouth and these two weren't stopped by the hail of bullets.

They both jumped in the air. The first took the

whole gun, hand, all the way up to the arm into its mouth

and decapitated it, leaving an open cavity gushing out

blood.

The second took his head and neck. As the headless

corpse dropped, all the wolves exploded into ashes.

Ivan kept on going backwards while listening to

Chloe repeated cries, "Oh my God what the fuck was that

oh my God."

He had to hear this all the way until he reached her

house.

Once she stepped out he took off with the back

door left wide open. He was terrified himself. He been a

witch hunter for fifteen years and knew for sure that what

he just seen wasn't witchcraft, but worse!

He quickly pulled over and made sure the camera

on his center rearview mirror caught it all.

He then plugged it into his phone and sent the

video to Sophia.

He then got back on the road, heading straight to

headquarters, which was eight blocks down the street in

the basement of the Bless Hope Church.

As soon as he entered the front door, the pastor

approached him.

"Sophia needs to see you immediately."

Ivan didn't bother asking why, he somehow knew.

He took the hidden downward circular staircase and once he reached the very bottom, he stopped at the metal door. He knocked two times. He softly counted to three and then knocked five times.

The door shrieked as it was opened from the other side. Ivan entered and immediately saw all the witch hunters sitting around a huge circular marble table. Sophia was sitting on a larger chair, straight ahead, "Please sit," she said to Ivan.

He walked to the only empty chair and sat and she began; "Eleven years ago, Pandora's Box was opened in the small town of Phillipsburg. Five demons were released, but only three were captured and placed back into the box."

She stopped talking while the marble table played the video Ivan's car had recorded.

"I believe we found one of those demons," she said and then pointed at Viola in the video, "I believe that's Ursula: Mother of demons."

"How do we put her back in the box?" Ivan asked.

"Cut off her head with the angel Gabriel's sword," she replied.

"And where do we find this sword?" He asked as the pastor walked with a long leather case.

He placed it on top of the table and opened it, revealing a titanium blade mid-evil sword with a gold-plated handle and large red ruby at the bottom.

The Viola in the video saw it and exploded into a thunderous shriek that shook the whole church.

Chapter 16

Jeff who was still locked up in his room, slowly decaying, heard Chloe come into the house.

"Daddy! Daddy!" She cried as she stormed up the stairs.

However, before she reached his bedroom door a swarm of crows shattered the window and spiraled around Jeff.

The crows carried him out of the window and all the way to Viola's house.

The front door opened and they carried him inside. They dropped him on the floor and flew in front of him to form Viola.

"You want the curse removed!" She scowled.

Jeff stood up and immediately a fly exited out his ear, "What do you think?"

Her eyes opened wide as they beamed a light onto the wall. Like a projection they displayed Gabriel's sword.

"Bring it to me and you shall be free of the curse,"

she said in her raspy high pitch voice.

"Now where do I find that shit at?" Jeff shouted.
Her eyes became normal and the projection disappeared. She burst into a mist and floated towards him becoming whole again two inches away from him and spitting blood onto his face. She then disappeared as the blood dribbled down his face and crawled up his nose.

"Follow the scent," her voice echoed in the room, "Take

Johnny's car is parked outside."

Chapter 17

Jeff did just that and as soon as he entered the car

this intense irresistible smell like a vampire scenting

blood and having the urge to quench it came over him.

It brought him to the front door of the Bless Hope

Church.

There the scent intensified and the urge to obtain

the sword became unbearable.

He stormed out of the car and walked to the door.

He pushed it and it wouldn't budge.

"Fuck! What now!" He screamed.

Then he heard a crow on the tree to the left say,

"Your dead and strong punch your way through!"

He watched it fly away into the distance and then

punched the door, braking all his knuckles.

Of course, he didn't feel anything because he was

dead so he punched it again, this time braking his wrist.

He examined his hand, he was amazed in how loose his

wrist was, causing his hand hang and stay downward.

So now he realized that punching wasn't going to

work, so he decided to charge at it with his shoulder.

The door shattered in half.

He crawled in and was immediately confronted by the pastor. "Excuse me! Stop right there!"

Jeff swung at him with the broken hand and ended up knocking him out with the wrist.

He then proceeded forward following the scent. It led him to a statue of Christ at the far end of the wall.

He stood next to it and the scent seemed to come from below it.

He leaned against it and pushed it to the side

revealing a hidden staircase. Within ten seconds he was

standing in front of the metal door.

With his good hand, he pounded on it while

shouting, "I'm here to make a collection."

As soon as he was done three flies came out of his

left ear.

He waited for a good five minutes and then

knocked again. Still no answer.

"What the fuck man!" He growled and was getting

ready to give up when all the sudden, he witnessed the

three flies crawl between the crack of the floor and door.

Once they got through, they each crawled into the ears of

three witch hunters.

Immediately their eyes became black.

Sophia and Ivan felt the dark energy's presence.

Ivan quickly grabbed the sword while Sophia

fought one of the three possessed witch hunters. While

she snapped his neck one of the other hunters opened the

metal door for Jeff.

Ivan saw this and positioned himself for battle,

while holding the sword upward. The third possessed

hunter grabbed him from behind and threw him against

the wall, causing him to drop the sword on the floor.

Out of nowhere a purple thick electric chain exited

out of Sophia's sleeve.

She threw like a rope while holding onto its end. It wrapped around the hunter's neck, who had opened the door for Jeff.

She pulled the chain toward her taking his head.

Meanwhile Jeff grabbed the sword and ran for the door while the third hunter distracted Sophia.

She wrapped the chain around his ankle and dropped him.

She retreated her chain and ran up the stairs after Jeff, whom was already in the car. As soon as she stepped out of the church a swarm of crows blocked her

way. They quickly formed Viola.

Chapter 18

Sophia quickly threw the chain at Viola. It wrapped around her wrist and she used it to pull Sophia towards her.

Viola then turned her free hand into a swarm of flies that rapidly formed the figure of a sledge hammer.

She banged Sophia's chest with it, attempting to send her back into the church, but Sophia pulled herself back using the chain still attached to Viola's wrist and collided both of her feet against her chest, pushing herself away again, but this time taking Viola's hand with her.

Viola exploded into a murder of crows and spiraled upward, while releasing a thunderous shriek. Then they came back down to form Viola whole again without missing limbs.

Sophia landed on her feet and swung the chain again at Viola.

Viola saw it coming and exploded into a dark cloud of flies.

Sophia saw this coming and reached inside her pant pocket and grabbed what appeared to be some type of black dust and blew it at the flies. The whole cloud became one big ball of fire. As the ashes rained onto the ground Sophia walked through them towards Jeff, but he was gone. Just then she saw the crow fly down the street.

She knew it was Viola, but didn't know where she was heading to. However, she knew who would.

Chapter 19

Chloe who was horrified from witnessing Viola take down Johnny, pounded on Jeff's bedroom door.

"Daddy please open up! Please!" She cried unaware that he wasn't in there.

But she was terrified, she needed him more than ever now! She kept on pounding on the door while increasing her cries. She finally got fed up and turned the knob.

She pushed the door open and was immediately sickened by the smell.

Meanwhile Jeff arrived at Viola's house. He entered carrying the sword just as the crow Sophia had witnessed also arrived. It flew by Jeff and stood in front of him. It slowly grew larger becoming Viola.

"Great job," she thanked in her raspy high pitch voice. She then reached for the sword.

"Not so fast," Jeff scowled.

She understood and slowly waived her hand in front of him.

"Is done," she said, however he didn't feel any different.

He looked down at his hands, they were still decaying.

"You didn't remove shit," he scowled.

"When you wake up tomorrow, you will be normal

again."

She informed, but Jeff wasn't convinced. He turned

around and headed towards the front door. Viola placed

her hand in front of her with the palm facing upward.

Immediately Jeff's body released a trail of grey sand that

entered her fingertips.

As more of his skin entered her fingertips, it

exposed his muscle. He noticed this and stopped walking.

He turned around to face her and she lowered her hand,

ending the collection.

"What the fuck are you doing to me?" He scowled.

"Just letting you know how easy I can kill you," she said in a deep tone of voice and then asked, "Now would rather me do that than remove the curse?"

Silence conquered the air and before he could respond she opened her mouth wide screaming, "Go home!"

The vibration was so intense, it caused him to drop the sword and fly out of the front door. It shut by itself as he landed on the black top. Of course he tried to get back in but the door wouldn't open. He then heard the crackling of the crow. He turned around to see it on top of the telephone pole. It made eye contact with him and then flew away.

Chapter 20

Jeff quickly jumped into Johnny's car and followed

the crow all the way to his house. It flew through his

shattered bedroom window. So, he parked the car stepped

out and rushed up stairs.

As he was going up he ran right into Chloe. Once

she saw his skinless body she exploded into screams and

pushed him.

He went backwards, rotating to his side. Once he

landed on the steps, he busted two ribs.

The force of the impact caused his head to move

upward and then jerking downward, snapping his neck,

in the same position.

Chloe just stood there frozen, but whimpering

what sounded like gibberish.

She watched him come to a stand and her

whimpering became louder and the gibberish faster.

Jeff noticed that his view of Chloe was sideways.

So, he grabbed his head and snapped its straight.

Now he stared at Chloe who was as pale as a blank page. He heard a tiny thunderous sound and looked down to witness her urinating herself.

It then hit him. His worse fears had come to play.

"Is me pumpkin," he abruptly said.

Just the sound of his voice made her shiver.

It didn't belong to the skinless body she was staring at.

Her whimpering now became a deafening extremely high pitch shriek.

"Is me," he hollered attempting to get through to her. However, it wasn't computing.

She was too paralyzed in fear to even understand it was reality.

As all of this transpired, the crow stood on Jeff's window sill and felt Chloe's weakness.

Viola the crow, tilted her head to the side feeling the roots she had place on Chloe growing into a tree and now a branch. Something useful to her. It jumped off the sill and grew larger in size, until the crow was Chloe size.

It crackled in a chanting rhythm, causing Jeff to now be paralyzed.

Chloe became silent. Her eyes rolled to the back of her head. She took three steps up and tilted her head towards the bathroom as though, she was looking at it, but in her warped mind she saw nothing.

She twisted her head to the opposite side now and saw Daddy's bedroom. She walked in and began undressing.

The huge crow allowed her to rest her back against

the bed. It watched as she grabbed the bottom of her

thighs and moved them upward, putting her feet all the

way up in the air.

The crow stuck its chin up, exposing its muscular

feathered chest while its beak pointed into the heavens. It

jumped on top of the bed. It brought it torso downward,

while keeping its chin up as it penetrated her.

One, two, three simple humps and it exploded into

dust, while Chloe remained there with her legs up and

feeling its semen bounce off the walls of her fallopian

tube.

Her eyes rolled back to normal as she felt the only

sperm penetrate her ovary.

Chloe all the sudden reappeared back in front of

her father's walking corpse and fainted.

Chapter 21

Viola stared down at the sword.

"I can't grab it," she said.

Then a deep tone demonic whisper replied, "Cause your still weak."

"Silence, Anukoora," she cried.

Then an eight feet tall shadow figure came out of the wall behind her.

She felt its presence and bowed down as it grew pierced red eyes.

"Do not challenge me for once I have my vessel I will grab that sword and cut off your head!" It said sounding only to her like cold whisper, causing her very skin to boil and end with blisters.

"I'm sorry, master."

As the shadow retreated into the wall it warned, "Prepare yourself they are here."

Sophia used her electric chain to slice the door in half.

As it collapsed, Viola saw Sophia and Ivan right behind it.

"Is too late witch," Viola growled and exploded into a murder of crows and reappeared in front of the sword, so Sophia wouldn't have easy access to it.

"You can't wield the sword, demon?" Sophia instigated.

This infuriated Viola, she placed her hand out with the palm facing upward.

Immediately, Sophia skin began to turn into dust and made its way into Viola's fingertips.

Anukoora came out of the wall and whispered, "Enough!"

Viola stopped and turned to face him as Sophia lacking the energy to stand, fell onto her knees.

"Why do you insist!" Viola challenged.

Anukoora, Prince of demons and keeper of chaos has never chosen a side, but his own.

As Viola was distracted by him, Ivan rushed in and grabbed the sword.

Anukoora saw this and allowed it.

Ivan brought the sword to Sophia. As soon as she grabbed it, she felt its energy run through her blood streams as it healed her.

Viola felt this and turned around to face her, then back at Anukoora.

"What have you done?" She scowled.

"You have served your purpose," he whispered, but all three were able to hear.

Viola quickly turned to face Sophia again, but this time felt the coldness of the blade slice open her neck. As she exploded into dust, Sophia dropped down to her knees while holding the sword in front of her as though she was offering it to Anukoora.

Ivan looked at her puzzled.

However, before he could say a word, she put the sword through his chest. Sophia then pulled the sword out of him and bowed down to Anukoora.

"You have done well," Anukoora whispered.

She didn't say a word.

"Now I need you to protect my vessel," he continued.

She glared at him. He could feel her anger towards him, but he knew she had no choice but to obey. Fighting him now would only result in her death.

He couldn't be killed with the sword at this period. But only when he entered his human vessel, would he be at his weakest.

All she could into then was obey and try to

keep order in chaos.

Meanwhile, Jeff awakened on his bed with the

curse removed and no memory of what transpired. As

with Chloe, but something was growing inside her and

she could hear it whispering......

The Darkest Hours III

The Whisperer Game